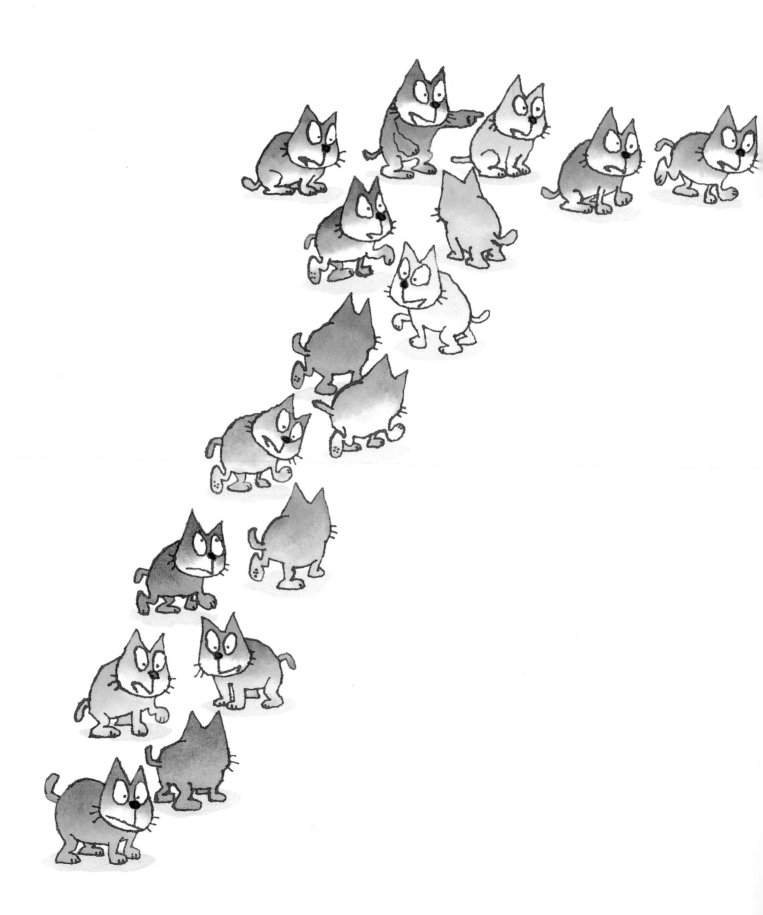

COMIC ADVENTURES OF BOOTS

First published in Great Britain in 2002 by Andersen Press Ltd., 20 Vauxhall Bridge Road,
London SW1V 2SA. Published in Australia by Random House Australia Pty., 20 Alfred Street,
Milsons Point, Sydney, NSW 2061. All rights reserved.
Colour separated in Italy by Fotoriproduzioni Grafiche, Verona.
Printed and bound in Italy by Grafiche AZ, Verona.

10   9   8   7   6   5   4   3   2   1

British Library Cataloguing in Publication Data available.

ISBN 1 82470 033 2

This book has been printed on acid-free paper

OPERATION FISH-BISCUIT

PLEASED TO MEET YOU, MADAM QUARK

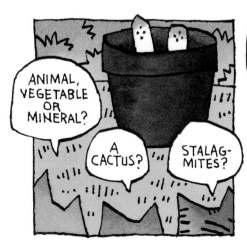